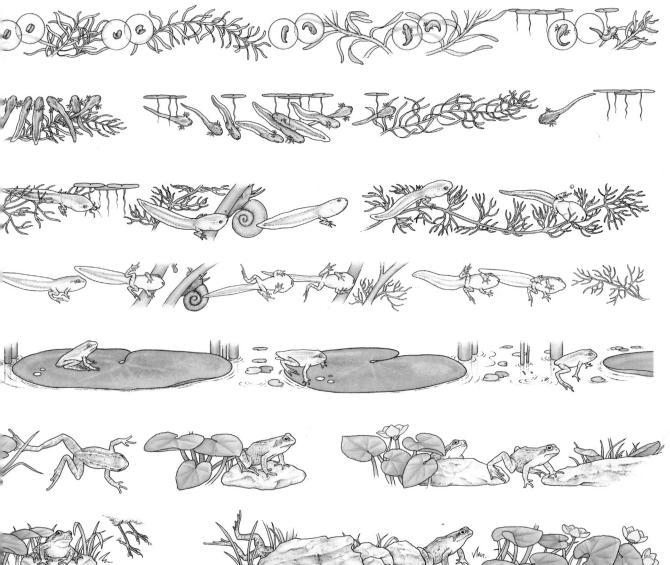

B. Thomas

CREATED BY DORLING KINDERSLEY

Library of Congress Cataloging-in-Publication Data

Taylor, Kim.
  Frog/photographed by Kim Taylor and Jane Burton.—1st American ed.
    p. cm.—(See how they grow)
  Summary: Photographs and text show the development of a frog from
the egg stage through over a year old.
  ISBN 0–525–67345–8
  1. Frogs—Juvenile literature. 2. Frogs—Development—Juvenile
literature. [1. Frogs. 2. Tadpoles 3. Animals—Infancy.]
  I. Title. II. Series.
  QL668.E2B86 1991
  597.8'9—dc20   90–43264
                                                              CIP
                                                               AC

First published in the United States in 1991 by Lodestar Books,
an affiliate of Dutton Children's Books, a division of
Penguin Books USA Inc.

Originally published in Great Britain in 1991 by
Dorling Kindersley Limited, 9 Henrietta Street, London WC2E 8PS

Printed in Italy by L.E.G.O.   ISBN 0–525–67345–8
First American Edition   10 9 8 7 6 5 4 3 2 1

Written and edited by Angela Royston
Art Editor Nigel Hazle
Illustrators Sandra Pond and Will Giles

Typesetting by Goodfellow & Egan
Color reproduction by Scantrans, Singapore

SEE HOW THEY GROW
FROG

photographed by
KIM TAYLOR
and JANE BURTON

Lodestar Books • Dutton • New York

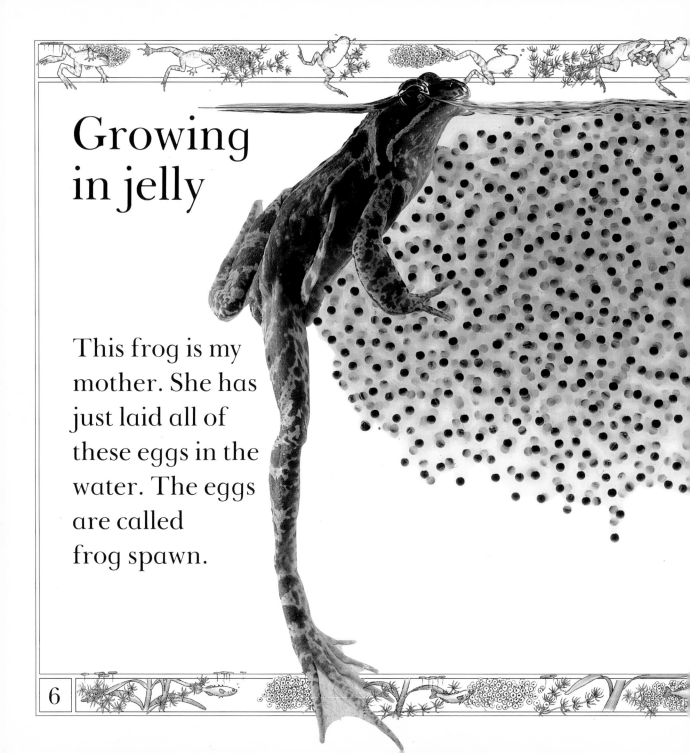

Growing
in jelly

This frog is my
mother. She has
just laid all of
these eggs in the
water. The eggs
are called
frog spawn.

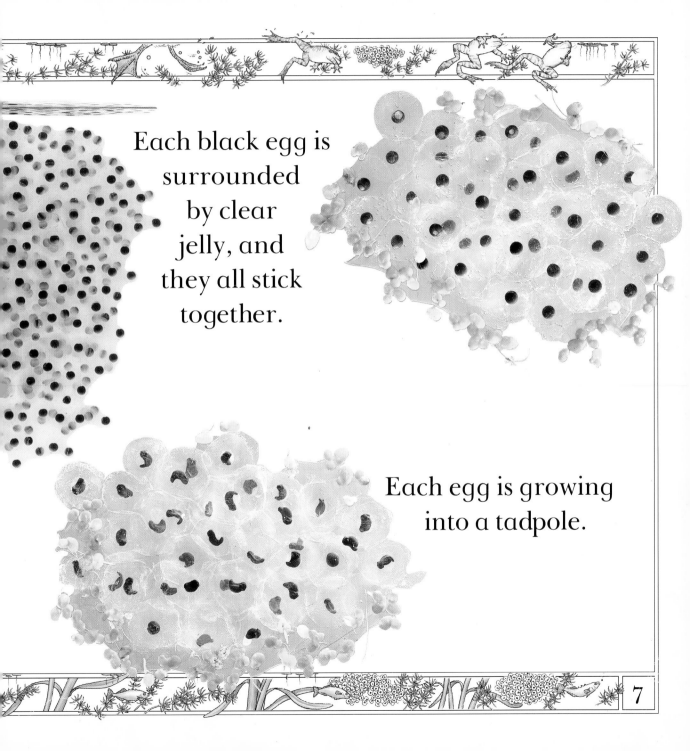

Each black egg is surrounded by clear jelly, and they all stick together.

Each egg is growing into a tadpole.

Just hatched

After two weeks,
I am ready to hatch.

Look at my long, feathery gills. They let me breathe underwater.

I push my way through the frog spawn and swim away.

9

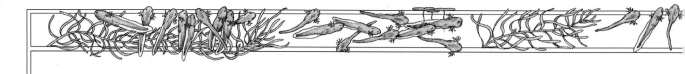

Tadpole

I am four weeks old now.
I like to swim with the
other tadpoles.

My gills have closed up.
I swim up to the surface
for each breath
of air.

I am growing bigger
and bigger. We all feed on
tiny, underwater
plants.

11

On my own

I am six weeks old now, and
I have grown much bigger.
I eat plants and insects
that fall into the water.

I like to swim on my own.
My back legs are beginning to grow.
I am slowly changing into a frog.

Getting stronger

I am nine
weeks old. I
am half
tadpole and
half frog.

My back legs are
growing longer, and now
my front legs are growing too.

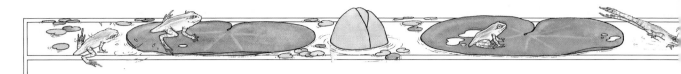

A frog at last

I am nearly twelve weeks
old, and at last
I am a frog.

I still have a long tail, which
helps me swim, but it is
getting shorter.

Here is a really
big frog. Look how
small I am beside her!

Out of the water

Now that I am more than one year old, I spend most of my time on land.

I sit quietly waiting for an insect to eat. Then I shoot out my long tongue and snap it up.

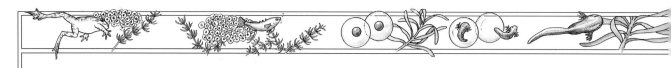

See how I grew

The egg   One day old   Four weeks old

Six weeks old   Nine weeks old

Over a year old

Twelve weeks old

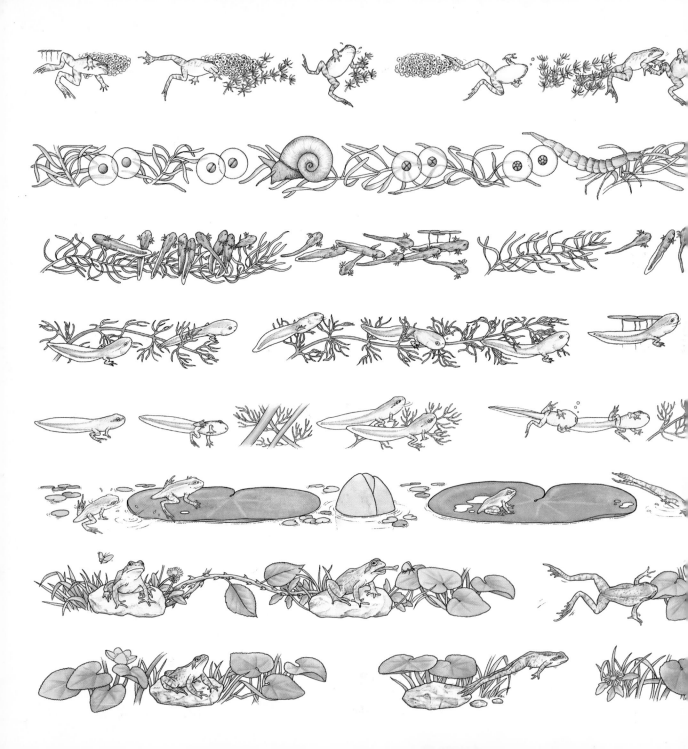

Shopkins™

Once you shop...You can't stop!

WELCOME TO SHOPVILLE!

By Jenne Simon

P9-DLZ-992

ISBN 978-0-545-84228-0

10 9 8 7 6 5 4 3   15 16 17 18 19/0

Printed in the U.S.A.   40

First printing, April 2015   •   Book design by Erin McMahon

Scholastic Inc.

Welcome to Shopville, the home of the Shopkins™! Apple Blossom, Cheeky Chocolate, and all their friends love to hang out at Small Mart. And today, they're competing in the Shopville Games. Check it out!

Once a year, the Shopkins show off their sporting skills during the Shopville Games! Here are this year's attendees:

Apple Blossom is juiced up and ready to go.

Cheeky Chocolate never breaks under pressure!

Spilt Milk will cream last year's records.

Lippy Lips has colorful cheers to encourage her friends!

Kooky Cookie doesn't crumble when the chips are down.

And Strawberry Kiss always gives her berry best!

The first event is the Shopping Cart Sprint. Spilt Milk wants to beat the record for the fastest dash down the aisle. "I'm feeling fresh and ready to race!" she says.

On your mark, get set, go! Apple Blossom and Cheeky Chocolate push Spilt Milk's cart down the aisle.

"Faster! I need to go faster!" cries Spilt Milk. "Team, I can taste victory, but I need your help!"

Spilt Milk's race crew won't let her down! But can they make it across the finish line fast enough?

The next event is the Popsicle Stick Chop. Cheeky Chocolate is nervous. "I've only ever broken through two sticks before," she says. "But this year I'm trying for three!"

"You can lick those sticks!" Lippy Lips cheers.

Cheeky is ready. She thinks sweet thoughts, jumps high in the air, and does her signature chocolate chop! "HI-YA!"

CRACK! All three sticks splinter right down the middle. "You've broken your own record!" cries Apple Blossom. Cheeky couldn't be happier. "Isn't life sweet?"

Next up is the Frozen Food Climb. Apple Blossom, Strawberry Kiss, and Cheeky Chocolate all race to see who can reach the top of Frozen Food Mountain in record time.

Climbing Frozen Food Mountain is hard work!
"If I weren't so cold, I'd probably melt!" groans Cheeky.

But Apple Blossom still has some juice left. With a burst of speed, she reaches the top and breaks the record!

"Deep down in my core, I always knew I had it in me!" she says.

The Checkout Jump is the final event. It's the toughest competition yet. Shopkins will be judged on the skill of their jumps over the checkout scanner . . . and their style!

Kooky Cookie is the favorite to win.

"She'll be one tough cookie to beat," says Apple Blossom.

FLIP!

But are they made
of the right stuff to win?

It's Kooky Cookie's turn. She gets a running start and soars into the air to swing from the banners. Round and round she goes, bigger and faster than anyone has before!

Suddenly, the banner breaks!
"Oh, no! My big flip is going to be a big *floooooop!*" cries Kooky.

But Kooky sails across the checkout scanner in a triple-twist flip. Everyone thinks it was part of her routine!

"That jump was just delicious!" Apple says.

"And it was a record breaker—you got the sweetest score ever for creativity!" says Cheeky.

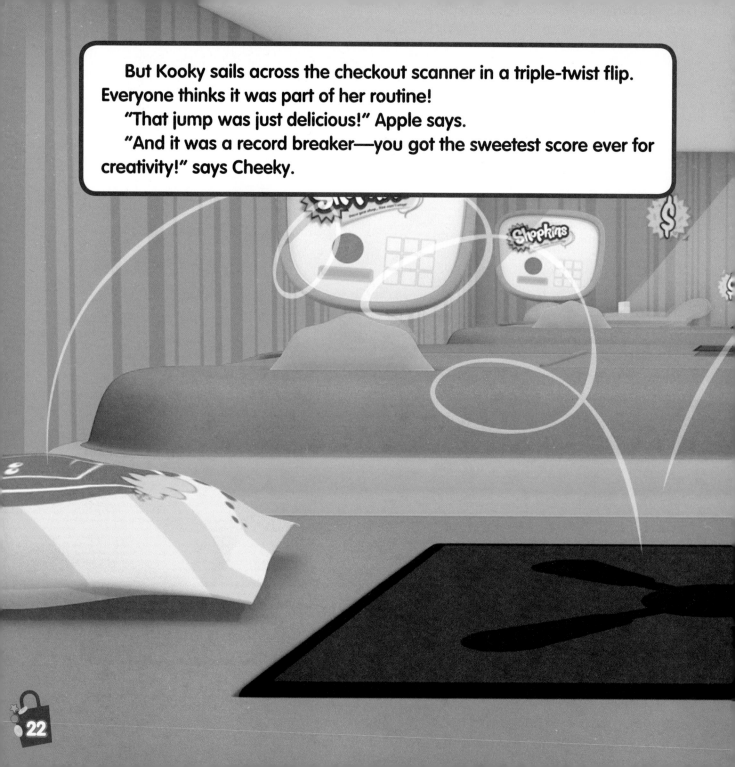

CHECKOUT JUMP!

The Shopville Games have been a huge success!
Because when you have friends like the Shopkins, everyone wins!